Winnie the Pooh
Baby Journal

A Disney Keepsake Book

Original title: *Winnie-the-Pooh Baby Book*
Copyright © 2000 Disney Enterprises, Inc.
Winnie the Pooh Baby Journal: A Disney Keepsake Book
Copyright © 2002 Disney Enterprises, Inc.
All rights reserved. No part of this book may be reproduced
or transmitted in any form or by any means, electronic or mechanical,
including photocopying, recording, or by any information storage
and retrieval system, without written permission from the publisher.
For information address Disney Press, 114 Fifth Avenue, New York, New York 10011-5690.

Printed in the United States of America
Based on the "Winnie the Pooh" works,
by A. A. Milne and E. H. Shepard

First Edition
1 3 5 7 9 10 8 6 4 2
ISBN: 0-7868-3368-8

Visit www.disneybooks.com

Winnie the Pooh
Baby Journal

A *Disney* Keepsake Book

NEW YORK

Waiting for You

Paste sonogram here.

Sonogram date .... Due date ....

Possible names ...*Kahlil Amir*......... ...*Kahlil*..................
........*Kehlani*................ ....

Mother's full name .... Age ....

Father's full name .... Age ....

First time we heard your heartbeat

....

4

Waiting for You

Our thoughts and feelings..
....
....
....
....
....
....
....
....

Paste photo of baby's mother and father here.

Baby Shower

Hosted by

....

Guests ....
....
....
....
....
....

Gifts ....
....
....
....
....

Food ....
....
....
....

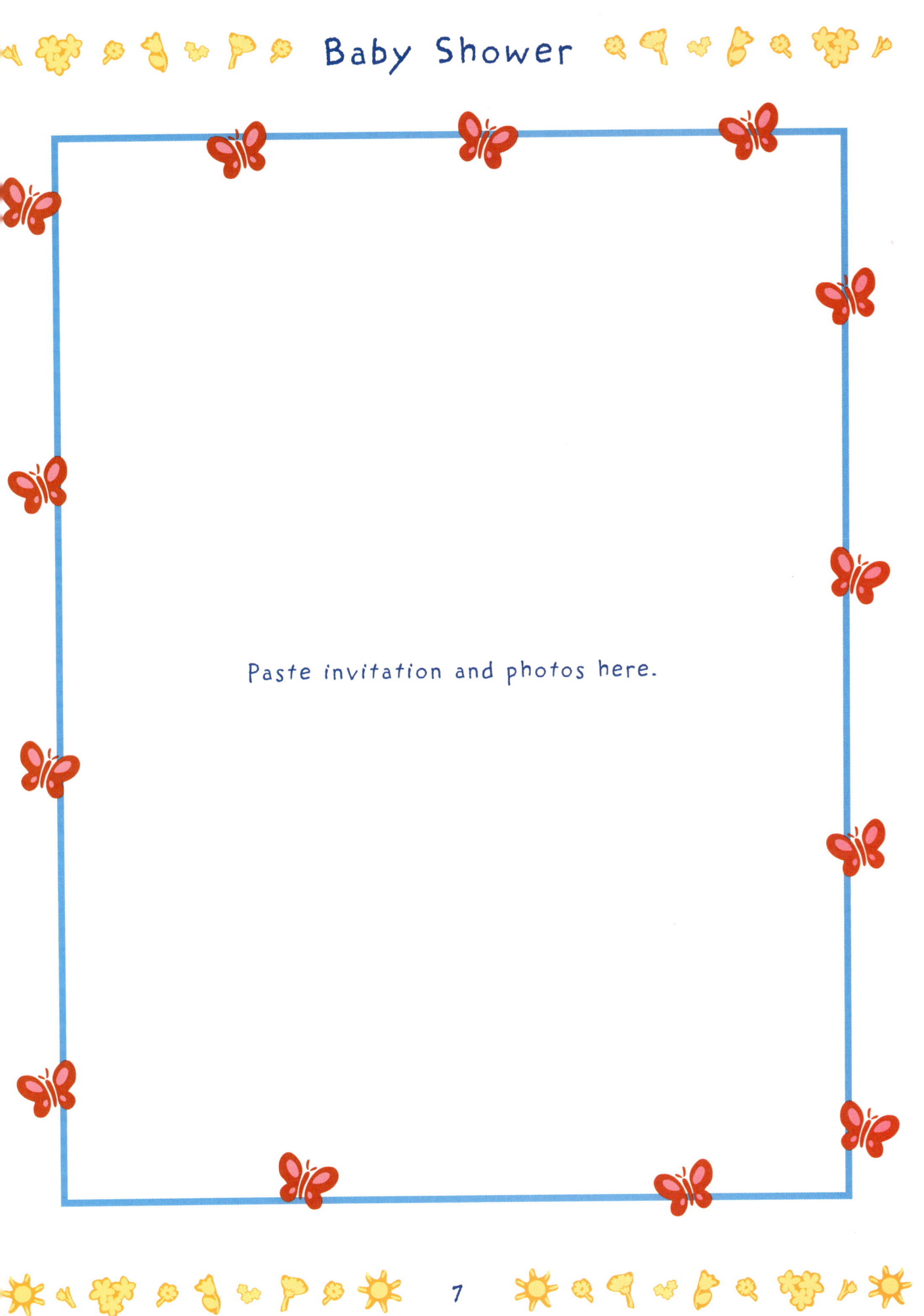

Baby Shower

Paste invitation and photos here.

Your Birth

You were born on..
    (month/day/year)

Your full name..

Your name means..

....

Time...

Date...

Place..

Weight...

Length...

Eye color..

Hair color...

You looked most like..

8

Your Birth

Doctor's name ....

Nurse's name ....

Visitors
....
....
....
....
....
....

Paste photo here.

Your very first photograph!

Things to Remember

Identity tag from hospital

Handprint

Footprint

Things to Remember

Paste baby announcement here.

Current events and other happenings on your birth date

....

....

....

....

....

Welcome Home

You came home on..

The weather was..

We live(d) at..

Special preparations for your arrival..................................
....

Your room was decorated with..........
....

Place photo of nursery here.

Your nursery

Welcome Home

Visitors ....

....

....

....

....

Special gifts

....

....

....

....

....

....

....

....

....

Your Family Tree

Paste family photo here.

My family

Your Family Tree

Mother's Side

Great-Grandmother
....

Great-Grandfather
....

Grandmother
....

Grandfather
....

Mother
....

Father's Side

Great-Grandmother
....

Great-Grandfather
....

Grandmother
....

Grandfather
....

Father
....

Siblings
....
....
....

Spiritual and Religious Ceremonies

Your special day was ....

Date .... Place ....

You wore ....

Family and friends who celebrated with us

....

....

....

....

....

Spiritual and Religious Ceremonies

Paste photo of
special celebration here.

The celebration

Your First Weeks

Paste photo here.

Wonderful you!

Sleeping schedule	Eating schedule
....	....
....	....
....	....
....	....

Your First Weeks

How you have changed ....

....

....

....

....

Your favorite activities ....

....

....

....

....

Bath Time

First bath at home..

First time in a big bathtub...................................

Favorite bath toys...

....

Favorite bath games...

....

....

....

....

....

Paste bath-time photo here.

All clean!

Bedtime

First slept through the night..

Favorite bedtime toys..

....

Favorite bedtime stories...

....

Favorite lullabies ....

....

Paste bedtime photo here.

Sweet dreams!

Mealtime

You first:

Ate pureed food

....

Ate solid food

....

Ate with your fingers

....

Held a spoon

....

Sat in a high chair

....

Drank from a cup with help

....

Drank from a cup alone

....

Ate a complete meal

....

22

Mealtime

Your favorite food(s).......................................
....
....

Food(s) you liked..
....

Food(s) you disliked..
....
....

Paste photo of baby eating here.

Yum! Yum!

Growing

Age	Weight	Length/Height
One month	....	....
Two months	....	....
Three months	....	....
Four months	....	....
Five months	....	....
Six months	....	....
Seven months	....	....
Eight months	....	....
Nine months	....	....
Ten months	....	....
Eleven months	....	....
Twelve months	....	....

Growing

Paste photo here.

You at .... months

Paste photo here.

You at .... months

Health

Immunizations	Age	Date
....	....	....
....	....	....
....	....	....
....	....	....
....	....	....
....	....	....
....	....	....
....	....	....
....	....	....
....	....	....

Teething

Your first tooth appeared on..

Your second tooth appeared on..

Your third tooth appeared on..

Your fourth tooth appeared on..

Paste photo here.

Your first tooth!

First Adventures

First time out in a carriage or stroller..

First time in a:

Car..

Train..

Bus..

Plane...

Paste photo of baby
on an outing here.

Special outings with:

Grandparents

....

....

....

Other relatives

....

....

....

Friends

....

....

....

Hello, world!

First Adventures

First vacation..

....

We got there by...

Favorite activity..

Place vacation photo here.

Your first vacation

Favorite vacation memories............................

....

....

....

....

Holiday Celebrations

Your first holiday

....

It was spent at

....

It was spent with

....

....

....

....

Paste holiday photo here.

Holiday Celebrations

Description of first holiday

....

....

....

....

....

....

....

Gifts you received

....

....

....

....

....

Your favorite gift was

....

Holiday Celebrations

Paste holiday photo here.

Holiday Celebrations

Paste holiday photo here.

33

First Events

First sounds

....

First smiled

....

First sucked thumb or pacifier

....

First held head up

....

Paste photo here.

Paste photo here.

First played with feet

....

First clapped hands

....

First grasped an object

....

First laughed

....

First Events

First rolled over

....

First sat up

....

First crawled

....

First stood up

....

First steps with help

....

First steps without help

....

First recognized your name

....

First word

....

First danced

....

First sang

....

Paste photo here.

First Events

First wore shoes

....

First walked outside

....

First waved good-bye

....

First had a haircut

....

First talked on the phone

....

First drew a picture

....

Paste photo here.

Making Friends

Paste photo here.

❀ You and ....

Things you liked to do together

....

....

....

....

....

First Birthday

Date ....

How we celebrated

....

....

....

....

Family and friends
who celebrated with us

....

....

....

....

....

....

Place first birthday photo here.

One year old!

First Birthday

Description of cake

....

You wore

....

Gifts

....

....

....

....

We gave you..

....

Favorite Things

Colors ....

....

Animals ....

....

Activities ....

....

Songs ....

....

Nursery rhymes ....

....

Toys ....

....

....

....

....

Favorite Things

Books ....

....

....

People ....

....

....

Games ....

....

....

Things to wear ....

....

....

What made you laugh ....

....

....

41

Special Memories

Paste photo here.

Date ....

Here are some of our favorite memories from your first year:

....

....

....

....

....

....

Special Memories

Funny things you said..
....
....

Paste silly photo here.

Silly you!

Special Memories

....

....

....

....

....

....

....

....

Baby's First Year Photo Album

0-3 Months

0-3 Months

0-3 Months

0-3 Months

0-3 Months

0-3 Months

3-6 Months

3-6 Months

3-6 Months

3-6 Months

6-9 Months

6-9 Months

6-9 Months

6-9 Months

9-12 Months

9-12 Months

9-12 Months

9-12 Months

9-12 Months